A Night at the FROST FAIR

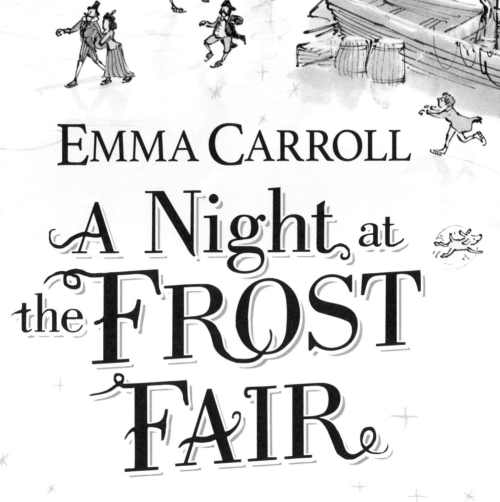

Emma Carroll

A Night at the FROST FAIR

ILLUSTRATED BY
SAM USHER

Simon & Schuster

FIRST PUBLISHED IN GREAT BRITAIN IN 2021 BY
SIMON & SCHUSTER UK LTD
TEXT COPYRIGHT © 2021 EMMA CARROLL
ILLUSTRATIONS COPYRIGHT © 2021 SAM USHER

THE RIGHTS OF
EMMA CARROLL & SAM USHER
TO BE IDENTIFIED AS THE AUTHOR AND ILLUSTRATOR
OF THIS WORK HAS BEEN ASSERTED BY THEM IN ACCORDANCE WITH
SECTIONS 77 AND 78 OF THE COPYRIGHT, DESIGN AND PATENT ACT, 1988.

1 3 5 7 9 10 8 6 4 2

Simon & Schuster Australia,
SYDNEY
www.simonandschuster.com.au

Simon & Schuster UK Ltd
1st Floor, 222 Gray's Inn Road
LONDON WC1X 8HB
www.simonandschuster.co.uk

Simon & Schuster India,
NEW DELHI
www.simonandschuster.co.in

CIP catalogue record for this book is available from the British Library.

HB ISBN 978-1-4711-9991-2
eBook ISBN 978-1-4711-9992-9 – eAudio ISBN 978-1-4711-9993-6

... characters, places and incidents are either ... tion or are used fictitiously. Any resemblance ... events or locales is entirely coincidental.

... BOUND BY BELL & BAIN

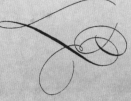

MIX
Paper from
responsible sources
FSC® C007785

For Abi E,
who asked for this story in the beginning
and blazed the way with kindness.

1

Leaving Gran was the hardest part. Harder, Maya thought, than seeing her in weeks-old clothes or finding a hairdryer instead of milk inside her fridge when they last visited her in her old house. They'd done the right thing, Dad said, as they left the care home. He said it again on the way to the station. And again as they waited for their train. Maya wasn't sure who he was really trying to convince.

She'd always had a special connection with her gran. It was a fierce, unspoken thing that didn't always make sense to her because they weren't the

1

slightest bit similar: Gran loved travel and exploring; Maya got queasy just from going to the supermarket in the car.

Right now, as she stared out of the taxi window, she felt angry, and sad. The people in the care home had seemed very nice, but something about the beige walls and furniture didn't feel like her gran at all. Her room was so small there wasn't space for all her things. They'd had to put the souvenirs from her many adventures into storage, and Gran had looked so lost without them.

It would've been easier if Mum was here to talk to, Maya thought. But she was in India visiting her sister.

Beyond the taxi window, darkness had turned the city into a sea of lights. It was raining. As the traffic crawled across London Bridge, cars stopped. Started. Stopped again.

Dad spoke to the driver. 'Reckon we'll make our train?'

Maya wasn't really paying attention.

Just before they left the care home, Gran had given

Maya and her older sister, Jasmine, presents, and Maya was using all her energy to hide her jealously towards Jasmine.

'These things are very precious to me,' Gran had said, pressing packages into their hands.

Jasmine's present was a gorgeous star-shaped brooch that came in its own red leather box.

When Maya unwrapped her own present, something brown and ugly emerged from the pale blue paper. She glanced at Gran, confused.

'It was Edmund's,' Gran whispered.

'Oh,' said Maya.

'Oh, Mum, not this Edmund again?' said Dad.

No one knew who 'Edmund' was, although Gran had been talking about him more and more recently. Gran said she'd met him on her travels, but beyond that she was pretty vague. They'd searched for clues in her old photographs and the other stuff she kept – the ribbons and bus tickets, coat buttons, birthday cards and wrappers from old chocolate bars – but none of it had led to answers.

'I thought you might be interested in Edmund, my dear,' Gran said, patting Maya's arm. 'You've got an explorer's mind inside that head of yours.'

'Have I?' said Maya, surprised.

Gran nodded. 'The world is full of things we've never seen or heard of, but they are there — sometimes we just have to go looking for them.' Maya felt she should understand what Gran was trying to tell her, but she didn't. And she couldn't help wishing that Gran had given her a pretty gift like her sister's, rather than a lump of who-knew-what. But she loved Gran and didn't want to hurt her feelings, so she thanked her for the present and stuffed it into her pocket.

Now, in the quiet of the taxi, Maya looked at the brown lump. She'd no idea what it was, and didn't see how it linked to this person called Edmund.

She slumped back in her seat. It was raining heavily,

the wipers swishing faster over the taxi's windscreen.
In the headlights of other cars, Maya saw flecks of
white. The rain was turning rapidly to snow.

A bit *too* rapidly.

She sat up, alert.

'What's going on with the weather?' she asked, but no one else seemed to have noticed.

And then Maya was no longer sitting inside a taxi.

She was standing in a busy street, shivering.

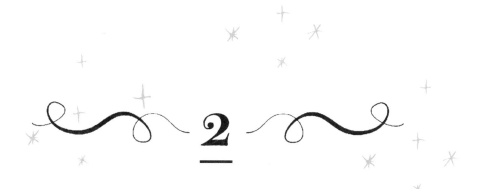

2

'**O**ut of the way, numbskull!'

Maya stumbled into the gutter just in time, as a cart pulled by horses thundered past. From the opposite direction came a man on horseback and plenty more people on foot. The taxi was nowhere to be seen.

I'm dreaming, Maya decided. *I've fallen asleep and in a minute I'll wake up.* At least she hoped she would. She started walking; it was the only way to get warm. The taxi must be here somewhere; she just hoped she was heading in the right direction to find it.

Quickly, the road became busier, till it was a heaving mass of people.

'Don't panic,' Maya told herself. 'Just go with it. It's only a dream. It'll be over soon.'

The road led under a huge stone arch and out onto a bridge, though not the same London Bridge as before – this one had even more people crossing it, and tall buildings on either side of the road. The only light came from fires in metal baskets that burned on the street. All around her, men, women and children surged forward in one excited mass of people. As Maya's eyes adjusted, she realized how oddly dressed they all were.

Halfway across the bridge by now, Maya grew steadily more confused. She passed pubs, a chapel, a steakhouse, pie shops and shoe shops, and a house advertising quiet rooms for ladies to rest and drink tea.

Stuffing her hands into her coat, Maya walked as fast as the crowds allowed. Her pockets, as usual, were full of tissues and sweet wrappers. Back in the taxi, Gran's present had been in there too: it wasn't now. But, she reminded herself, she was dreaming. And odd things always happened in dreams, though this one felt more vivid than usual . . .

Then, through a narrow gap between the buildings, Maya glimpsed the river. She was amazed. There were things on the river that definitely weren't boats. Things with legs that shouted and waved.

People.

From north bank to south, the river was completely frozen over.

She'd never seen the Thames like this: actually, she'd never seen a frozen river before – only in films and those ones were probably computer-generated.

This didn't look anything like a movie, though. It looked real. It felt real, just as the cobblestones and the snowflakes did. She kept walking, keen to get to the other side of the bridge. Passing under another archway, she found herself on the opposite bank of the river.

The second her feet touched solid ground again, she knew. No, this wasn't a dream. She didn't understand what was happening, but she was seized by a sense of purpose, as if she was here for some sort of reason.

At the water's edge were signs advertising a fair. Some of the lettering was hard to read, but the parts she could sent excitement shooting through her:

ONCE IN A LIFETIME EXPERIENCE!
MEET MR JACK FROST!
EAT, DRINK AND BE MERRY AT TONIGHT'S
MARVELLOUS FROST FAIR ...

'A shilling a go on the ice, ladies and gents!' said the man collecting people's payments. 'More chance of me turning into King George than of that ice cracking.'

King George? Maya thought. *That can't be right. We have a queen, not a king.*

She rubbed her eyes. Nothing changed.

Something very odd had happened back there in the taxi. And now she was in olden-times London. She – Maya Mulligan – had somehow time-travelled all the way to the past.

'A shilling,' the man said to Maya, holding out his hand.

'But I haven't got a shilling.'

'No money, no ice,' said the man. 'Hop it.'

Maya backed away. She didn't have the foggiest idea what a shilling even looked like. She'd walked a few steps when someone with very cold fingers grabbed her wrist.

'Help me. Please, I beg of you.' As the crowd shifted sideways, a boy of about her age emerged. He looked very pale. Very scared. 'You've got to help me. Someone's following me.'

'Let go of me. NOW!' Maya yelped. The boy looked strange to her, his eyes were a bit too big and bright for his face. The purple coat he wore flapped about his legs like one of Gran's old dressing gowns.

'If I'm with you, it'll throw him off the scent. He won't expect me to be with . . .' The boy eyed Maya's jeans and trainers suspiciously, clearly finding her as odd as Maya thought him. 'A girl.'

'You'd better let go of me, I'm warning you,' she snapped.

With a quick glance over his shoulder, the boy dropped his hand.

'Please, will you help me?' he begged.

Maya scowled, rubbing her wrist. 'Why would I want to help you?'

'A man in a dark cloak is following me.' The boy's

17

eyes darted everywhere as he spoke. 'I've escaped for now, but he'll stop at nothing to get me back.'

'Really?' Maya folded her arms. It sounded like the plot of a cheesy film.

'Really, truly,' he replied. Then he grinned. 'I say, you're rather feisty for a girl, aren't you?'

Maya glared. 'I'm not the one asking for help,' she reminded him.

He smiled again, which made him look slightly less odd, and – in a way Maya couldn't put her finger on – almost familiar.

She shook her head. She'd walk away. Get on with what she was here for and not be dragged into his problems. The trouble was, she didn't know why she was here, somehow in the past. She only knew that she wanted to go to the frost fair. And that she was still standing, rooted to the spot, not walking away from the boy at all.

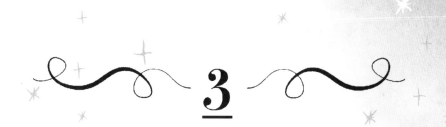

3

From the river came the sounds of whooping and laughing, and music from somebody's fiddle. Dogs were barking. Horses neighed. A whole world was going on out there on the frozen Thames: a strange, magical world.

'Listen,' Maya said, looking the boy in the eye. 'I don't know how much help I'll be to you . . . Oh.' The boy held up two small silver coins between his thumb and forefinger.

'Shillings,' he said. 'You need to pay to go on the ice.'

Maya paused. 'You're offering to pay for me?' she asked.

'Of course.' The boy gave a little bow. 'These frost fairs only happen every twenty or thirty years. So I pulled out all the stops to get here tonight. But as soon as they know I'm missing, they'll come looking for me,' he explained, his mood darkening.

Maya chewed her lip. If the boy was telling the truth, the idea of being followed made her uneasy. But if she wanted to get onto the ice, she needed this boy as much as he needed her.

'So if we could hurry, that would be wonderful,' said the boy.

'All right,' she agreed. 'But any sign of trouble, I'm off.'

The boy grinned.

'Here, catch!'

He flicked a shilling up into the air. Maya caught it squarely with her palms.

'What's your name, by the way?' the boy asked.

'Maya,' she said, pocketing the coin. 'What's yours?'

'Eddie.'

'Where first?' she asked.

'The terrier races,' Eddie decided.

They followed the sound of yammering dogs to a spot right in the middle of the river, where a large crowd had already gathered.

'Folks bet on the dog they want to win,' Eddie explained.

As they watched, a dozen manic little dogs tore down the track. What they were chasing, Maya couldn't see, but it sent them all crazy. The race ended with a pile-up of wriggling, squirming dogs. The winner was a tiny white terrier that panted so much it seemed to smile. Maya laughed hard, and so did Eddie, though it set him off coughing.

'Where next?' she asked.

Eddie scanned up and down the river. There was so much to choose from: skittles, card tricks, skating

and dancing. His gaze came to rest on something to Maya's right.

'We absolutely HAVE to go on those!' he cried. 'Come on!'

Linking arms, they hurried over to a spot where a circle of torches stood upright in the ice. Inside the lights was a pair of brightly painted swingboats.

Eddie had already found his way to the front of the queue and was waving at her.

'Hurry, we're next!' he yelled.

Moments later, they squeezed into what looked like a rowing boat. The seats were wooden benches, the floor slushy-wet wooden planks.

'Hold on tight!' Eddie insisted, as they started to rock.

The movements were gentle at first. Then, with more force, they swung backwards. The swingboat went high – so high Maya feared they'd flip right over. For one long second they hung in mid-air, before plummeting downwards.

Down and down they went. Then up and up and up again.

When the swingboat finally slowed and stopped, Maya was one of the first to get out.

'I'm glad that's over,' she said, clutching her stomach.

Eddie swayed as he stood up. 'That was wild, wasn't it?'

But the look they shared said neither of them had had enough, not when there were so many other stalls to look at.

After the stalls, they played skittles very badly, then stopped to hear a fiddler play toe-tapping tunes, and joined in by singing along.

Maya hadn't had so much fun in ages.

Yet once they'd lost another penny on a buns-in-the-jar game, Eddie fell oddly quiet.

He tucked his arm through hers and hurried her away, not stopping at the next stall. Or the next. He ploughed on through the crowds.

'Hey! What's the rush?' she cried, tripping and sliding as she tried to keep up. Reluctantly, Eddie slowed to a walk.

'I saw the man who is following me. Things could turn nasty so you'd better go.'

'Go?' she said, startled. 'I'm not going anywhere.'

Something had changed between them in this last hour or so. She no longer doubted he was telling her the truth, and that was because they had become friends. And friends believed each other and didn't leave each other when the trouble started.

As they reached a stall selling coffee, Eddie stopped again.

'Maya,' he said quietly. 'Don't look. Don't point. Just stick with me. And RUN LIKE MERRY HELL!'

4

Eddie charged straight for the crowds. Maya kept on his tail as best she could.

They took a sharp right between two food sellers. It brought them out at the back of the main row of stalls. Instantly, it was quieter and darker.

Eddie didn't stop until he'd reached the opposite riverbank. There were stone steps leading up from the river, the type used by people getting on and off boats. Maya expected Eddie to bound up them onto dry land. But a fit of coughing caught him.

'Have we shaken him off?' she asked.

Eddie nodded, unable to speak. Now, for the first time, Maya noticed how skinny he was. He looked flushed and feverish, though not from the exertion of running.

'Who exactly are we running away from?' Maya demanded.

But Eddie's face was closed: very clearly he wasn't going to talk about it.

'You're ill, aren't you? You should be in bed,' she said, realizing.

'That, my dear Maya, is exactly why I'm here.' Wearily, Eddie rubbed a hand across his face. 'Having freedom makes me feel so much better – people need freedom to breathe.'

To Maya, though, he looked very pale. 'I think you should go home,' she muttered. *Home.*

Thoughts of Dad and Jasmine flashed into her mind. She didn't know how this time-travel business worked exactly, but she hoped her family weren't 200-odd years away, wondering how she'd disappeared from the back of a stationary taxi.

'Eddie, perhaps we should—' She stopped.

Standing, just a few metres away on the ice, was a man in a dark cloak and hat, his eyes fixed on Eddie.

'Uh-oh,' she said under her breath.

Grabbing Eddie by the arm, they dodged round the man so fast it took him by surprise.

'Back towards the swingboats,' said Eddie, fighting for breath.

Yet as they wove between the stalls, he kept stumbling and slowing down. Finally Eddie begged her to stop. 'Just till I get my second wind.'

Another coughing fit tore through him. Maya wondered how much longer they could keep running.

'Better?' Maya asked hopefully as Eddie straightened up.

He wiped his mouth. 'Thank you, yes. Though we can't come to the frost fair and not buy a souvenir.'

'But we need to keep moving,' Maya reminded him.

'The seller's right there,' he insisted, pointing to a stall surrounded by customers.

'The best gingerbread in the whole of London!' the woman serving it shouted. 'Get your slices here!'

Gingerbread seemed an unusual souvenir to Maya, but Eddie was already heading to the stall, so she followed.

'How much you having, ducks?' the woman asked them, knife hovering over a tray of cake. The cake smelled delicious – toasty and fruity. The look of it made Maya start. It was square-cut, dense, brown and familiar. But it couldn't be, could it . . .

'A brick-sized piece, if you please,' Eddie said.

Around them, as the crowd shifted a little, Maya

caught sight of a man in a black triangular hat. Her chest tightened in panic.

'We need to go, Eddie,' she urged.

'You want it wrapped? And there's to be writing?' the woman asked.

Eddie nodded. Deftly, the cake was wrapped in blue paper and tied with string.

'Come on, come on,' Maya hissed. The man was advancing towards them.

Then the woman handed the package over, with a pen.

'We haven't got time!' Maya cried. 'Hurry!'

But a sort of calmness had come over Eddie. As she hovered at his shoulder, he took the pen and wrote on the package. She glanced at the man. Then at the pen moving over paper.

'Hurry up, Eddie! Please!'

She seized his sleeve. Her feet were sliding, though not in the right direction. Someone else had hold of Eddie now, dragging him away with such force Maya couldn't fight back.

'I've found you,' the man cried. 'At last.'

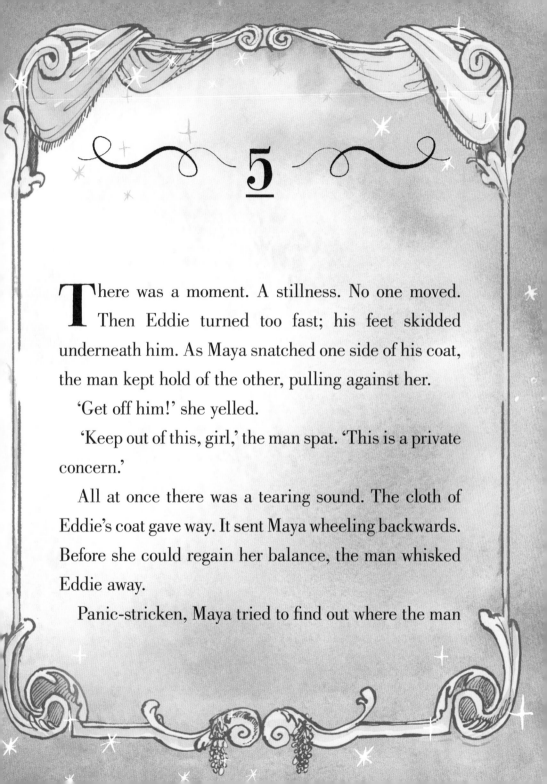

5

There was a moment. A stillness. No one moved. Then Eddie turned too fast; his feet skidded underneath him. As Maya snatched one side of his coat, the man kept hold of the other, pulling against her.

'Get off him!' she yelled.

'Keep out of this, girl,' the man spat. 'This is a private concern.'

All at once there was a tearing sound. The cloth of Eddie's coat gave way. It sent Maya wheeling backwards. Before she could regain her balance, the man whisked Eddie away.

Panic-stricken, Maya tried to find out where the man

and Eddie had gone. She asked stallholders, sellers, random passers-by, but no one had seen them. No one seemed to care much either. People were still whooping in the swingboats, still buying gingerbread.. How could they carry on as normal? How could they not want to help?

Maya headed in the direction of the riverbank. Beneath her feet, the ice had begun to turn grainy. Water seeped into her socks so when she walked it made a squelching sound. She was tired. Whatever this experience was, she'd had enough of it. She needed to work out how to get home. But she also knew she had to find out where the man had taken Eddie. She couldn't leave without knowing if he was all right.

Climbing the river steps, she came out onto a busy street. The air smelled different, she noticed – not of cold any more, but of the city starting to warm up, like old, forgotten fruit at the bottom of her school bag. It had started to rain.

The shouting didn't register at first. It was coming

from a side street somewhere to her right.

'I won't go inside again!'

With a jolt, Maya recognized the voice. She also knew the dark, spindly outline of a boy in a flapping coat, wrestling with someone on the pavement.

'Let go of me!'

'Quiet!' said the man. 'Enough of this ridiculous noise!'

Maya raced down the street towards him. 'Eddie!'

At the sound of her voice, he looked round. The tiniest distraction was all it took. In one sly move, the man grabbed Eddie's arms and bundled him up the steps and inside. As Maya reached the building, the front door slammed shut.

She banged her fists against the door. 'Eddie? Are you in there? Answer me!'

There was no reply.

Eventually, she backed down the steps and gazed up at the house. She was surprised by how ordinary it looked. It wasn't how she'd imagined a prison to be.

She went to the door again and thumped on it.

'I'm not going away until this door is unlocked. I'll stay here all night if I have to!' she yelled.

A little way along the street an upstairs window slid open. A lantern appeared, followed by woman's white-capped head.

'You won't keep up this hollering till morning, will you?'

Maya stared at the woman.

'Because we all need our sleep, my dear – your friend Eddie especially.'

'You know Eddie?' Maya rushed to the lady's window. 'He's been kidnapped! We have to do something!'

The woman actually laughed. 'Kidnapped? Good gracious! Why on earth would you think that?'

Maya frowned. 'He told me … he's being kept prisoner!'

'My dear,' the woman said patiently. 'Eddie doesn't like being kept inside, but it's doctor's orders.'

'Doctor's orders? He said this place was a prison.'

'It probably does feel like a prison to him.'

'But the man who came after him,' Maya insisted. 'Eddie said he'd stop at nothing to get him back.'

The woman sighed. 'That man, my dear, is Eddie's father.'

Now Maya was completely confused.

'His father,' the woman repeated. 'Is at his wits' end. Young Eddie won't accept how ill he really is. A congestion of the lungs, so they say.'

So Eddie hadn't been kidnapped after all – not properly, anyway. In fact, this business with his lungs sounded more of a danger to him.

Maya had an idea.

'Have you got a pen?' she asked.

The woman pulled a face. 'You'll be wanting the inkstand too, will you?'

'A pencil, then. And some paper, please?'

Moments later, both dropped from the window to land on the pavement beside her. Using her leg to rest

41

on, Maya scribbled a note – not to Eddie, but to the man who was his dad. She thought it might be harder to ignore than a knock at the door, and it was the one thing she could think of that could help. It might be hopeless, but she had to try.

With the note delivered, Maya headed back towards London Bridge. The rain was falling harder now, but at least no one could tell that she was crying. She felt sad for Eddie, and was cold and tired, and worried she might be stuck here forever if she couldn't work out how to get home.

The bridge, as before, was heaving with people. But this time, instead of barging into her, they seemed to melt away as she walked.

Up ahead, she saw two red lights glowing through the rain.

It was a taxi, sitting in traffic with its engine running. More incredibly, it was her taxi – she recognized the adverts for West End shows all along its sides, and almost cried out with relief. Climbing inside, she flopped down on the back seat.

'A really weird thing's happened,' Maya began, but her sister, Jasmine, was listening to her music, oblivious. Dad was still talking to the driver.

Her family hadn't realized she'd gone.

Maya noticed, too, that her hair was now dry, her trainers no longer squelchy-wet.

Had it all been a dream as she'd originally thought? Had she actually gone anywhere at all?

'Ouch,' she muttered, as something hard dug into her hip. In her coat pocket, she found the funny brown lump Gran had given her. She took it out, turning it over in her hands. Funny, but it really did look familiar.

6

Back home, Maya still didn't understand what had happened, but was beginning to see that Gran's present had a very big part to play in it. In the bright light of her bedroom – and to her huge surprise – she realized the brown lump was, in fact, old gingerbread. She also noticed something written on the tatty blue paper it was wrapped in. Though the ink was faded, she could just about make out the words:

This piece of gingerbread
was bought at the frost fair
on the Thames,
5th February 1788,
by Edmund Mulligan.

Maya's jaw dropped.

So Eddie was Edmund!

Maya scrambled about for her phone. She had to speak to Gran right away.

'Have you asked your father if you can use the phone?' Gran barked on hearing Maya's voice.

'It's my mobile,' said Maya, trying to stay patient. It had taken her ages to find the care home number and get transferred to Gran's room, and now she was desperate to find out what her grandmother knew. 'Listen, it's about that present you gave me today.'

'Edmund's gingerbread?'

'Yes, Eddie . . . I mean . . . Edmund.' It felt funny to call him that. 'Can you tell me some more about him?'

'I'm tired,' said Gran tartly. But Maya knew she was just testing her out, seeing how much she really wanted to hear about the person no one else believed existed.

Maya tried again. 'That thing you said today about the world being full of stuff we don't understand – well, I took your advice and went looking for it.'

A pause, then Gran simply said, 'Good.'

'The present was wrapped in blue paper, and it's got writing on it,' Maya went on. 'It says Edmund's full name. He was a Mulligan, wasn't he? Just like you were before you married Grandad.'

At the other end of the phone, Gran took a deep breath. 'He was my father's great-great-great-granduncle – too far back for anyone to remember. But somehow that piece of gingerbread got passed down through our family. No one really wanted it, but it fascinated me, so I did a bit of research into Edmund.'

'And?' Maya asked eagerly.

'Poor lad, he was mollycoddled terribly by his family. They never let him do anything. Something to do with his lungs.'

'Did he . . . Did Eddie die?'

'Of course he did – dear, dear me.' Maya heard the smile in Gran's voice. 'But not in 1788.'

Maya's stomach did a swoop of relief. 'What happened to him?'

'Well, he was quite a character, was Edmund. He kept on escaping from the house and going on wild capers across London. Eventually, his father realized that shutting him away only made his son's health worse.'

Maya grinned down the phone. She could absolutely imagine Eddie being a handful.

'The final straw was when he escaped to go to a frost fair on the river. It was all very public, his father catching him and forcing him home again in front of crowds of people at the fair. Someone wrote a letter to the family, asking that he stop keeping Edmund inside like a prisoner. That he be allowed to have adventures like other children.'

'Really?' Maya gulped. 'Did it work?'

'Amazingly, it did. And what do you know? Eddie got better. He lived to a ripe old age, made happier by living it the way he wanted.'

'I'm so glad,' Maya said.

'People need their freedom, Maya. They need to breathe,' Gran whispered.

People need their freedom. They need to breathe.

A lump grew in Maya's throat. Those were Eddie's words. She'd borrowed them herself to write that note, and now Gran was using them too. She glanced at the gingerbread, still there in her other hand. It had made its way through the family in pretty good shape for a 200-year-old piece of cake. So had those words about freedom. They were, Maya realized, a sort of souvenir themselves.

And that something was Gran. Eddie's story ended happily after all; Gran's story, though, felt like it might need a little bit of help.

Maya went downstairs to where Dad was still skyping Mum.

'We've done the right thing,' he was saying.

'You don't sound very happy about it,' Mum remarked.

'Hi, Mum.' Maya waved at the screen and held up the gingerbread.

'Hi, sweetheart.' Mum blew a kiss. 'What on earth is that?'

Maya took a deep breath and began to tell them about Eddie.

The next weekend Gran moved to a different care home.

This one had a library full of books and old maps on

the walls. And Gran's room was big and airy with plenty of room for the souvenirs from her adventures.

'A home fit for an explorer,' Gran said. 'Though I'm more the armchair variety nowadays.'

'You've still got an explorer's mind,' Maya reminded her. And she understood now that she did too.

From the care home lounge, there were views across the Thames. It didn't freeze over, not even in winter – those days were long gone. But in summer, when all the windows were open, Maya would sit with her gran and they'd stare out at the water. Often, they'd talk about Edmund.

And sometimes – just sometimes – when the breeze blew off the river, they'd smell something spicy, like gingerbread.

THE END

AUTHOR'S NOTE

There's something truly magical about a frost fair. It's been over 200 years now, since the last frost fair was held on the Thames. Pictures of it show people having a wonderful time playing games, buying food, enjoying the strange spectacle.

Even at a time when winters were colder and the Thames more likely to freeze, frost fairs weren't common. If you were lucky enough to go to one, it was important to buy a souvenir. Items like engraved spoons, or printed tickets, or certificates were very popular. So too was gingerbread.

My idea for this story came from an exhibition held at the Museum of London Docklands in 2014 to mark the anniversary of the last frost fair. On display was a piece of gingerbread from 1814, hard as a rock and wrapped in pale blue paper.

I wondered how the museum had got hold of that piece of gingerbread – had someone donated it to the museum? Had it been hiding in an attic for years? Was it an heirloom passed down through a family?

It was this last idea I liked best. Frost fairs were all about escaping, celebrating and having fun, despite the terrible cold. When Maya travels back in time, she sees how important it is to have fun, even when life can feel like winter.

FROST FAIR
FACTS:

The period from the 1300s to the 1870s was known as the little ice age because winters were much colder.

During the little ice age the Thames froze on at least twenty-four occasions.

Old London Bridge, which was made of nineteen arches, slowed the river, making it more likely to freeze.

Boatmen who ferried people across the Thames, and couldn't work when the river was frozen, converted their boats to sledges.

At the 1814 fair, an elephant was led across the river.